Mermaid Island

Suzanne Weyn

PRICE STERN SLOAN
Los Angeles

For Maggie Stovall
with love

Published by Price Stern Sloan, Inc.
11150 Olympic Boulevard
Los Angeles, California 90064
ISBN: 0-8431-3619-7
Printed in the United States of America

10 9 8 7 6 5 4 3 2 1

Contents

Island Paradise

"This is so beautiful," Barbie sighed dreamily as she stepped off the plane. A warm, tropical island breeze ruffled her long blond hair. All around, palm trees swayed in the gentle breeze and colorful birds flitted from tree to tree.

"This is only the airport," Ken said as he stepped out of the plane. "Can you imagine how great the rest of this island must be?"

"I can," said Kira, who was behind him.

Coming out of the plane behind Kira were Teresa, Christie, Christie's boyfriend Steve, Midge and her husband Alan and Barbie's cousin, Jazzie. "Too bad Skipper had school," said Barbie. "She would have loved this."

After picking up their baggage inside the airport terminal, the gang went outside to find a cab. They were also looking for Alex, a friend who was a native islander. They had met Alex while he was living in America. Alex had returned to his island home, but the gang had kept in touch with him through letters.

"Look for Island Cab twelve," Steve told the others. "That's the cab Alex drives."

"There's twelve," said Barbie. The gang picked up their suitcases and went over to the number twelve cab.

"Where can I take you folks?" asked the cab driver. He was *not* Alex.

"Sorry," said Barbie. "We thought Alex drove this cab."

The driver shook his head. "Alex doesn't drive a cab anymore."

"What?" Christie exclaimed in surprise.

Just then, the sound of a horn honking made the gang turn. Not far from them was a tall, good-looking, dark-skinned man. "Alex!" Alan cried happily as the gang rushed over to him.

"Aren't you driving a cab anymore?" Midge asked.

Alex smiled proudly. "No more," he said. "I have a new business now. I am the owner of a new glass-bottom boat, the *Island Lady*. I take island visitors out to see the wonders of the fish and coral under the sea."

Barbie hugged him. "How wonderful!"

"Thank you," said Alex.

"I don't think we'll all fit in the jeep," Jazzie pointed out. "Why don't Teresa, Kira and I take a cab?"

"What's your address?" asked Kira.

"Just say you want to go to Alex's house. He'll know," Alex said as he helped Ken and Steve load up the luggage into the back of the jeep. "And tell him not to charge you."

In minutes, the gang was off, traveling along the narrow, twisting island roads.

"It was so generous of you to invite us all to stay with you at your house," Barbie told Alex.

"The more the merrier," Alex replied. "You were all so kind to Winnie and me when we were in America. I'm glad to be able to return some of your hospitality."

"How is your daughter?" Midge asked. "She must be very different from the last time I saw her."

It seemed to Barbie that a shadow of sadness passed across Alex's face. "Yes, she's changed," he said. "Winnie was only eight when we came back to the island. She's a lovely young lady of sixteen now."

"Sixteen," Christie said with a fond laugh. "Smiling Winnie with the long, skipping legs and braids is a teenager now. Imagine that."

Alex pressed his lips together tensely and nodded. Barbie wondered what was bothering him. She was sure something was wrong.

They drove through the town with its elegant shops and restaurants. When they turned a corner at the end of town, Barbie heard the sound of crashing waves. "Do you live by the water, Alex?" Barbie asked.

"Not far from the boat marina where my new boat is docked," he said. "It's perfect. There is a pink coral beach behind the house and I can see the marina from my front porch."

Before long they came to a simple, square, one-story house of light green with gleaming white shutters and an open front porch. "This is home," said Alex, pulling into the driveway.

The gang unloaded their bags and carried them into the house. "Winnie," Alex called.

"Where is that girl?" asked Christie. "I can't wait to see her."

Barbie was looking out the back window, when a loud bump and the sound of Christie's gasp made her turn.

In the doorway was a beautiful dark-skinned girl of sixteen sitting in a wheelchair. Barbie recognized the girl's beautiful amber eyes and her delicate features.

It was Winnie!

2

Visit to Mermaid Island

"It was a car," Alex explained sadly during lunch on the back porch. "The driver was going so fast that he knocked Winnie right off her bike. The driver didn't even stop."

Christie put her hand on Winnie's shoulder. "This must be hard on you, isn't it?"

Winnie attempted a smile, but her eyes were sad. "It hasn't been much fun," she said.

"But Winnie will walk again," said Alex. "The doctors say that with a lot of exercise, Winnie will be back on her feet in about six months. She's worked with a therapist for three months now, so she's halfway there."

"If you believe the doctors," Winnie said doubtfully with a glum shrug.

"Of course you can believe the doctors," Barbie said, smiling. "I remember you as a very determined girl, Winnie."

"Want to see the island?" Alex suggested.

"We'd love to," said Ken, clearing away the lunch bowls. "And I want to see your boat."

The gang took the short walk to the marina where Alex's boat was docked. "It's a beauty," said Alan as they climbed aboard the large white boat which seemed to glisten in the sunlight. "But I don't see a glass bottom."

Barbie spotted what seemed to be a door in the boat's floor. "Is that it?" she asked.

"Yes. I'll open it when we get a little deeper," Alex explained. Soon they were traveling through the clear, aqua-blue water. Barbie realized that the sun was strong. She didn't want to get burned, so she took out her new glitter sunscreen.

"Wow, that really makes you shimmer and shine," Midge said as Barbie spread the lotion on her arms and legs. "You look great."

Barbie tossed her the tube. "Try some."

Midge applied the lotion and held up her glittering arms to admire their shine. "You always find the fun stuff, Barbie."

Barbie smiled. Then she leaned over the side to look at a small island in the distance.

"That's Mermaid Island," Alex said. He turned the boat in the direction of the island and soon they could see it more clearly. Its shore shone with pink sand and the shrubs behind the narrow beach were a tangle of low, flowering trees. A few feet offshore, Alex shut off the boat. "This is a perfect spot." He pulled back the door on the boat's floor, revealing a glass bottom. The gang gathered around and peered down at the colorful world beneath them. Yellow-striped angel fish passed, followed by dazzling multi-colored rainbow fish.

The sea creatures darted in and out of pink coral ridges. Exotic purple underwater plants spread out like fans. "It's like a magical world under there," said Barbie. "I almost wouldn't be surprised to see a mermaid swim by."

"It's interesting that you say that," Alex told her. "This island is called Mermaid Island because long ago it was believed that mermaids lived among these coral beds. Of course, it was only a myth, but a lovely one." Alex sighed and looked out to the ocean sadly. "If only real life could be as carefree as a mermaid's life."

After two hours of sightseeing, Alex returned them to the dock. After dinner he excused himself and went to his small office. "I have a lot of bookkeeping to catch up on," he said.

Winnie said she was tired and went to bed. The gang walked down to the beach to watch the setting sun. "Does Alex seem very sad to anyone else?" Barbie asked.

"It must be because of Winnie," Christie said. She's not the same happy girl I remember. Poor Alex. It was so hard on him after his wife passed away, too."

Barbie nodded. "I hope she'll come out of this all right. I'm tired," she said. "I'm going to bed."

"I'll go with you," said Christie. Together they walked to the house and went in the back door. "Look, Barbie," said Christie, nodding toward Alex's office.

Through the open door, they saw that Alex had fallen asleep with his head on his desk. "Let's wake him and send him off to bed," Barbie suggested." But as they entered his office, Christie brushed against the corner of Alex's desk, knocking papers onto the floor.

"Look at these," Christie said as she knelt to gather up the papers.

"Christie, we shouldn't read his papers," Barbie said, kneeling to help her.

Christie didn't listen to Barbie. Instead she kept looking at the papers, and her eyes filled with concern. "These are unpaid bills," she whispered. "This one is from the bank. They are going to take back *Island Lady* unless he pays them. This is terrible! Alex's new business is failing!"

3

Barbie Takes Action

"I see you have uncovered my unhappy secret," said Alex, coming out onto the porch the next morning as the gang was eating breakfast.

"I'm sorry," said Christie. "I knocked over the bills and I couldn't help but see."

"Yes, this morning I noticed the bills were out of order," Alex said. "I figured out what must have happened. It's all right that you know. This way I don't have to pretend everything is fine."

"Can we help?" Barbie asked.

Alex shook his head. "I must make a payment on my boat by next week. If I don't, the bank will take it and I'll be out of business. I don't think I will be able to make the payment."

"That's terrible," said Midge.

"It is," Alex agreed, "but the only extra money I have must be spent on Winnie's therapy. As it is, I have cut her back from going twice a week to only going once."

Barbie propped her chin on her hands and thought hard. There had to be some way they could help Alex. "Do you have any idea why business is so bad?" she asked him.

"There are too many other tour boats already in business," he explained. "They are more well-known than I am."

Barbie stood up. "Then we'll have to make you more well-known."

"What do you have in mind?" Ken asked.

"We need to do a little advertising," said Barbie. "Alex, could you drive us into town before you start your day's work?"

"Certainly," Alex agreed.

Alex drove Barbie and Ken into town. "Drop us at that art supply store, please," Barbie said. Alex stopped at a blue store with a bright green awning. "Thanks," said Barbie. "We'll find our way back."

With a wave, Alex pulled away. "What do you have in mind?" Ken asked as they entered the store.

"Some creative sign-painting," Barbie replied. She picked out paints in bright colors, brushes and ten large pieces of poster board.

When they got outside, Ken looked around for a cab. "Let's rent motor scooters." said Barbie. "Everyone seems to drive them. I noticed a rental place down the block."

Barbie and Ken walked to the rental place and rented two scooters. Ken selected a red one, and Barbie picked one in bright pink. "I haven't ridden one of these in a while," said Barbie as she fastened her pink helmet. "I'd better practice a bit in the parking lot, first." Barbie found that she remembered exactly what to do. After making a few practice circles, she and Ken were ready to go out onto the road. With her art supplies tied onto the back of the scooter, she headed toward the marina. Ken was right behind her.

Barbie loved the feeling of the warm island air in her face. She would have loved to ride all around the island. But she couldn't. She had important work to do.

When they reached Alex's house, the gang was waiting. "What's the plan?" asked Jazzie.

"We're going to make signs about Alex's business, and put them all over the island," said Barbie.

"Great idea!" cried Kira. "Let's get to it."

They took the art supplies out on the back porch. "All right," Midge said. "What do we write?"

"'Come down to the *Island Lady* at the marina for a great time,' and then give the times the boat goes out," Ken suggested.

"All right," Midge agreed. But just as she and the others were about to begin painting, Barbie stopped them.

"Wait!" she said. "Why don't we give a free

concert right in front of the *Island Lady*? We can hand out flyers telling everyone about the *Island Lady* tours."

"That's brilliant!" said Jazzie. "People are sure to come down to hear free music. And once they're right there, they might as well take a tour. The more people who take tours, the more people will tell others."

"Midge? Christie? Did you happen to bring your guitars?" Barbie asked.

"I did," said Midge. "I thought we might want to have a sing-along on the beach."

"Me, too," said Christie.

"Then all we need to do is get hold of some tambourines and maracas," said Barbie.

"Alex has a steel drum," said Steve. "We used to play together. I bet he'd let me use it."

"All right!" Barbie cheered. "We're in business. Let's start making those signs. This will be a concert this island won't forget!"

4

Shocking Surprises

"Put your hands together and clap," Barbie told the crowd that had gathered by the *Island Lady* for the free concert. Barbie danced along the low wooden platform the gang had built on a grassy area near the boat.

Barbie was proud of how fast they'd pulled this concert together. In town, the guys had found matching tropical-print shirts which they wore with white pants. The ladies wore unmatched tropical shirts with white shorts. They'd even come up with a name. They called themselves Island Beat.

As the crowd clapped along, Barbie sang a song with a Caribbean beat. Behind her, Midge and Christie played guitar, Steve played steel

drum, Teresa hit a tambourine and Jazzie shook a pair of colorful maracas.

The night before, Ken and Alan had gone to a local club and talked the owner into renting them some microphones. Now Ken and Alan stood behind Barbie and sang harmony.

The crowd applauded and cheered when the song was done. Then Barbie began to sing a gentle, wistful island song called "Yellow Bird." The crowd swayed in time with the music.

As Barbie sang, she looked out into the crowd at Alex and Winnie, who were handing out flyers telling people all about the *Island Lady* tours. Midge, with her neat handwriting, had written them up. Kira had even taken a photo of the boat which she had developed in a one-hour developing place. She put the photo on the ad and then photocopied over a hundred copies. Barbie was very pleased with the way it had turned out.

"Thank you all for coming," Barbie told the crowd when she had sung her last song. "Before you leave, I hope you all sign up to take an island tour on the *Island Lady*, the finest glass-bottom boat you'll find anywhere. Just talk to Alex, that gentleman standing by the boat. You'll have a great time."

Barbie and the gang waved to the crowd, which continued clapping. "Well," Barbie said, turning to her friends. "That was certainly a success."

"I thought I'd cry when you sang 'Yellow Bird,'" said Midge. "It was so beautiful."

"Thanks," said Barbie. At that moment, she felt great. But her smile faded as she noticed that the crowd was breaking up without signing up for a boat tour. A few people walked by the boat, but even they didn't sign up. Barbie went over to Alex. "Did you get any customers?" she asked.

"Five, so far," he said. "Everyone likes a free concert, but I guess that doesn't mean they want to pay for an island tour."

"Don't give up," said Barbie. "We'll buy more art supplies and make more signs."

"Hold on," said Alex. "All of you worked so hard on this concert. I say you deserve some fun. After all, this *is* a vacation and you haven't even gone snorkeling yet."

"That would be fun," Barbie agreed. "I need to think and sometimes I get my best ideas while I'm swimming."

Although they were disappointed that the concert hadn't brought in more business, the gang agreed there was no sense feeling glum.

They went back to the house, changed into their bathing suits, gathered the snorkeling masks and flippers they'd each brought and headed down to the boat. When they got to the dock, Barbie noticed that three couples she'd seen at the concert were there. "Six customers are better than none," said Alex, coming up behind her.

Barbie smiled, but she knew six customers weren't nearly enough.

On the boat, Barbie sat on the front deck and let the spray of the salt water cool her. Beside her sat Winnie, whom Alex had lifted from her wheelchair. "My father has a lot of money problems, doesn't he?" she asked Barbie after the boat was under way.

Barbie nodded sadly.

"I didn't realize it until the concert today," said Winnie. "I suppose my doctor bills haven't helped matters."

"You can't blame yourself," said Barbie. "What happened wasn't your fault."

Winnie looked out to the ocean and sighed. Barbie wished there was something she could do for Winnie as well as for Alex.

Soon the boat slowed down near Mermaid Island. While Alex showed his customers the underwater world through the glass bottom of his boat, the gang put on their masks, breathing pipes and flippers. One by one they splashed into the water.

Barbie was the last to jump in. Instantly, she was amazed at all the fish she could see so clearly through her mask. The quiet beauty of this world made her forget, for the moment, all the problems she'd been working to find solutions for. Instead, she let her mind wander as she followed a brilliant green and blue parrot fish on its way along a peachy-colored coral reef. She was so intent on following him that she didn't realize she'd wandered quite a bit away from her friends—nearly to the other side of Mermaid Island.

Suddenly, Barbie froze. A black creature with a flat body and wide, bat-like fins had darted out from behind a rock. Its beady black eyes were fixed on Barbie—and she had no idea what to do.

5

Underwater Friends

A sharp tap on her shoulder made Barbie whirl around under the water. Behind her was Alex in his snorkeling gear. He swam several feet away and then held out his hand to the creature. Barbie watched in amazement as the fearsome-looking creature swam up to Alex and seemed to eat something from his hand.

Barbie swam to the surface and, in a moment, Alex came up beside her. "They're manta rays," Alex explained as he took his breathing pipe from his mouth. "They're harmless if they're not bothered. But I thought they might scare you, so I came around to see if they were bothering you for food."

"What are you feeding them?" Barbie asked.

"Conch," he answered. "They love it. It's an island shellfish. I've been feeding them for years. Even before I bought the boat I would often come out here and feed them."

Soon about ten of the black, kite-like creatures came silently gliding around them. Alex reached into the net bag he had tied onto his arm and handed Barbie some of the smooth, white conch meat. "Do you want to try?"

Barbie conquered her fear and took the conch from him. "Just hold it out and they'll come get it," said Alex as he popped his airpipe back into his mouth.

Putting back her pink air pipe, Barbie went back underwater with Alex. Her hand trembled just slightly as she held it out to the first ray she saw. She was amazed how velvety the ray felt when it glided past her leg. With a quick nibble, it took the conch from her hand.

Delighted, Barbie swam to Alex and got more conch from him. They spent the next half-hour happily feeding the rays. By the time they were out of food, Barbie no longer thought of the rays as creepy or sinister. Now they even looked cute to her and she thought of them as new friends.

When they were out of conch, Barbie and Alex came to the surface. "I'd better get back to my customers," said Alex. Together they swam toward the boat and found the others, including the six customers, excitedly snorkeling around the island.

"Look at this!" said Midge, swimming up alongside Barbie. She held out a handful of flat, round, snowy-white shells. Each shell was about the size of Midge's palm. "These sand dollars are lying all over the bottom of the sea."

"They're pretty," said Barbie, taking one of the smooth shells from Midge. "They look like they could be mermaid money."

"What a cool idea," said Midge. "Wouldn't it be nice if you could just pick money up off the ocean floor?"

"It sure would be nice for Alex right now if he could do that," Barbie agreed with Midge.

After another hour of snorkeling, Alex called them all back to the boat. He drove the boat back toward the main island and pulled in at a long, pink-sand beach. "Supper comes with the tour package," he told the group.

The gang and the customers got off the boat. Barbie saw a small wooden cottage with long picnic tables set up in front of it. The sign in front read, "Angel's Food."

"Have a seat," Alex told them. He went into the cottage and soon came out with a beautiful black woman with long black hair. "This is Angel," Alex introduced the woman to the group. "She makes the finest fried grouper on the island."

"What's grouper?" Ken asked.

"An island fish. You'll love it," said Angel as she returned from the cottage and placed wooden plates and silverware on the table.

As Alex had predicted, the gang ate a great meal. "I pay Angel to feed my customers," Alex explained as they ate. "She started this business when her husband passed away five years ago. She's done well."

When it was time to leave, Barbie saw Alex offer to pay Angel. Angel waved his money away and just went back into her cottage. "She is a wonderful woman," Alex said coming to Barbie's side. "She said to pay her after Winnie is done with the doctor."

"That's kind of her," said Barbie.

Alex nodded. "I want to ask Angel to marry me. We've been dating for three years. But I keep waiting for my business to pick up. I must have something to offer."

"You will," Barbie assured him.

"By next weekend I may have nothing at all," he said, shaking his head. "I don't see how I can possibly get enough money to pay the bank."

Barbie put her hand on his shoulder. "Maybe business will get better."

Alex smiled sadly. "It can't possibly get better fast enough to save my boat."

Alex drove the group back to the island marina. "Tell your friends about this tour," said Christie to the six customers.

"Oh, we will," one woman answered.

They walked back to the house as the sunset bathed everything in pink and gold. Barbie covered a yawn with her hand. "All the sun and excitement has made me tired," she said.

The gang went out onto the back porch to play a game of cards. "I'll pass," said Barbie. She headed out to a net hammock slung between two palm trees in the backyard. Crawling into it, she was quickly asleep. And soon she was in the middle of a dream.

6

The Dream

Barbie's dream was so real. In it, she was a mermaid! She was under the warm ocean and, although she had no snorkeling gear, she was breathing perfectly. She looked down at her legs. They were gone! In their place was a shiny pink tail with glistening fins. As her hair floated about her, she saw that it had lovely streaks of pink, green and blue in it.

Delighted, Barbie swam in a circle, laughing gleefully at how well her strong fins let her move in the water. Then, a sound made her turn. A whole group of beautiful mermaids were swimming toward her.

As they got closer, she saw who the mermaids were—Midge, Christie, Jazzie, Kira and Teresa. They, too, had rainbow hair, but their fins were a shimmering green.

In the dream, Barbie joined her friends and they swam happily together through the warm waters. A school of angel fish swam by, tickling them with their delicate fins. Then the rays joined them. Barbie reached out and petted their velvety fins.

Suddenly, the sound of high-pitched squeals filled the water. Barbie knew it was the call of dolphins. Barbie and her friends swam toward the sound, over coral reefs and dipping down into underwater canyons. After a short while, a dolphin swam up to them. "Follow, follow," he said. Somehow, in her dream, Barbie could understand him.

They followed the lone dolphin until he brought them to an entire pod of waiting dolphins. "Climb on," said the dolphin. Barbie and her friends grabbed hold of the dolphins' dorsal fins on their strong backs.

The dolphins took off at lightning speed. Barbie gasped in wonder as they leapt above the waves. She could see that they were near

Mermaid Island. She saw Angel and Winnie, on the island, waving to them. Mermaid Barbie waved back just as the dolphin plunged back into the water.

Finally, the dolphins stayed on the surface in a small silent cove. In front of them was a boat, half-sunken into the water. "Oh, dear!" Barbie gasped. It was the *Island Lady*!

Barbie watched in horror as the boat leaned onto its right side. Then, with a lurch, the boat sunk lower until it slipped under the water entirely. Barbie and the mermaids ducked below the surface and watched the boat tumble into a deep underwater canyon.

Quickly, the mermaids and the dolphins swam to the boat. They swam inside and looked around. The boat was empty. Barbie pulled open the door that covered the boat's glass bottom. Instead of seeing the glass, Mermaid Barbie saw a sign. It read: Something Special! Hurry! Not Much Time Left!

At that point, Barbie's eyes snapped open and she awoke. Slowly, she realized her adventure had been just a dream. She could see the gang still playing cards on the porch.

Sitting up, she thought about the dream. What had it meant? Something told Barbie there was more to this dream than just a fantasy. Suddenly a great idea came into her head. "That's it!" she cried.

Barbie hurried out of the hammock and ran up to the porch. "Barbie, what's wrong?" Ken asked. "You have such a strange look on your face."

"I had the most amazing dream," she said.

"Was it a scary one?" Teresa asked.

"No, it was a terrific one," Barbie said.

At that moment, Alex came out onto the porch, pushing Winnie in her wheelchair. "Terrific dreams seem to be part of the island's charm," he commented. "Many visitors report having lovely dreams."

"Listen to me," said Barbie excitedly. "The dream gave me an idea how to save your boat."

"What?" Alex cried softly.

"I know this might sound a little wild, but hear me out, you guys," said Barbie. "Alex's problem is that there are a lot of other tour boats on the island, right?"

"Right," Jazzie agreed for the group.

"Well, then," Barbie continued. "Alex's business might grow if he had something unusual to show to the public. What if they got to see mermaids through the bottom of his glass-bottom boat?"

"That would be wonderful," said Kira. "Especially for people with kids."

"Of course it would be terrific," Alex agreed. "But there's not much chance of that happening. Where would I find mermaids?"

Barbie gave him a brilliant smile and spread her arms wide toward her friends. "You're looking at them," she said.

7

Mermaids

Barbie ran down to the beach behind Alex's house. Her friends were in a circle of beach chairs with yards and yards of shiny green material spread out around them. Winnie sat in her wheelchair, sewing along with the others. "Wait until you see what I found," Barbie said excitedly when she reached them.

"What now?" Kira laughed. "Wasn't it enough that you found this great shiny green material for making fins?"

Barbie pulled some thick sponges and colorful jars from her bag. "This is hair color. You sponge it in, and it won't come out in water unless you use shampoo."

Midge picked up one of the jars. "This is green, Barbie," Midge pointed out.

"I know," Barbie said with a laugh. "The other ones are pink and blue. In my dream, we had rainbow streaks in our hair, so I thought it might be fun. No one else has to use the coloring, but I'm going to."

"I think it would be cool," said Kira.

"Too bad we couldn't find pink material for your fins," said Jazzie. "Then it would be *exactly* like in your dream."

"That's all right," said Barbie, sitting down on the sand. She picked some thread from Winnie's sewing basket and began stitching up the seam of a fin suit. "When these are done, we should get out to Mermaid Island and start practicing as soon as possible."

"I hope we can swim in these," Teresa worried.

"I'll be watching as a lifeguard," said Ken who knelt on some scrubby beach grass and cut material for a costume.

"Alan and Steve are on the *Island Lady* right now hooking up a stereo system so we can play music with our act," Christie told Barbie.

"I recorded your concert," said Winnie. "So you can use that music. I'm so glad you are all here. It's been so boring since I got stuck in this wheelchair."

"How is your therapy coming along?" Barbie asked her.

"Slowly," said Winnie. "The doctors want me to start swimming again, but it all starts to feel pretty hopeless. How can I go swimming when my doctor bills have almost ruined Dad? Besides that, he was going to ask Angel to marry him before this happened. Now he feels he can't ask her when he has a crippled daughter and not much money."

"Maybe things will be looking better soon," Barbie said hopefully.

When the costumes were ready, everyone took a ride out to Mermaid Island. Alex put down anchor at a deep spot close to Mermaid Island. The girls giggled as they wiggled into their mermaid-tail costumes. "This feels funny," Kira laughed, hopping across the boat in her costume as if she were in a sack race.

"We'll use our snorkel masks and airpipes to start," said Barbie. "Then once we know what we're doing, we'll do without them. Remember, when you need to breathe, come up close to the front of the boat so no one will see you. If you need help at any time, give a thumbs down."

Barbie put on her snorkel mask and airpipe. Then she sat on the edge of the boat. "Here goes," she said as she let herself fall into the water.

At first Barbie felt strange trying to swim in the fins. But, as her friends plunged into the water all around her, she slowly got the hang of it. She found that by kicking both of her legs at the same time and using her arms, she could swim pretty well.

It took about a half-hour for Barbie and her friends to feel really comfortable in the fins. When they did, they began to work on an underwater ballet. They came together in a circle, holding hands and then all arched backward into a back flip.

When Barbie needed air, she came to the surface close to the front of the boat. Ken leaned over the side of the boat. "Looking good," he told her. "I've been watching through the glass bottom. Look what we rigged up for you." He rolled a large silver tank to the side of the boat. It had a nozzle on top. Attached to the nozzle was a long rubber hose. "It's an air tank," he explained. "It will shoot air down constantly. It will let you mermaids take a quick breath without coming all the way up."

Ken gave Barbie some diver's tape and told her to tape the tube to the side of the boat. She did and then surfaced. "Would you see if Alex has any conch meat?" she asked.

Ken went to ask and returned a moment later with a string bag of conch. "Here," he said, handing the bag down to her.

Barbie dove down and swished the bag in the water. Soon the manta rays began to show up looking for the food. Barbie fed the rays, then gave some conch to each of her friends. Seeing that Barbie wasn't afraid of the rays made her friends brave. They fed the rays until the conch was gone.

"That was super great!" said Ken when Barbie and the others came to the surface. "Seeing a bunch of mermaids feeding those rays looks like something out of a fairy tale."

"Good," Barbie said with a smile. "That's exactly what I wanted."

8

A Change of Plans

"This is so exciting," said Christie on the day of the big show. Barbie, Christie, Jazzie, Midge, Teresa and Winnie were all out on Mermaid Island waiting for the *Island Lady* to come into view.

"The signs you all made were great," said Winnie as she did a last-minute repair on one of the costumes. "The boat is completely full today for the first time."

"If this show is a hit, it'll be full every day," said Midge, sponging colorful streaks into her auburn hair.

"It will be a hit," Barbie said positively. "An unusual show, topped off with Angel's great cooking, and the customers will have a day they won't ever forget."

"Speaking of cooking," said Jazzie, frowning. "I ate some french fries in town this morning that didn't agree with me at all."

"What's wrong?" Barbie asked. "Does your stomach hurt?"

Jazzie winced in pain and rubbed her stomach. "I'm afraid it does."

"You can't swim, then," Barbie insisted. "A stomach cramp could land you in big trouble underwater."

"But we promised a show with five mermaids," Jazzie insisted. "I can manage."

"No, you can't," said Barbie. "It's too dangerous."

"All our routines are for five mermaids," Jazzie argued. But then she bent forward and shut her eyes. "Maybe you're right, though. This stomachache is getting worse."

"Let me take her place," Winnie spoke up.

"What?" Kira questioned.

"I can swim like a fish," said Winnie. "I haven't tried to since the accident, but I don't see why I couldn't. The doctors say I should swim. My arms are strong, and none of you are using your legs much in those costumes."

"We're kicking with our legs," Teresa reminded her.

"I can use my hips and stomach muscles to get through the water," said Winnie. "I know the moves from watching you practice."

"Let's give it a try," Barbie said. "We'll get you into a costume and take a test swim."

Jazzie wriggled out of her costume and handed it to Barbie. Barbie helped Winnie into the costume, then wheeled her into the shallow water. She helped Winnie out of the chair and into the water.

Using her arms, Winnie worked her way out deeper. Barbie stayed right beside her the whole time.

At first Winnie splashed and her head slipped under the gentle waves. She came up spitting water and gasping. I hope I'm doing the right thing, Barbie thought as Winnie floundered.

"Want to go back?" she asked Winnie.

Winnie shook her head as she wiped water from her eyes. "I can do it."

"Take it slowly," Barbie cautioned.

Winnie took a deep breath and then plunged under the water. Barbie was right there with her. Winnie stroked and used her hips to move herself forward in the aqua-blue water. Within twenty minutes, she was swimming so well no one would have guessed she couldn't walk.

"So? What do you think?" Winnie asked Barbie as she came to the surface. Barbie realized that this was the first time she'd seen Winnie smile since they'd arrived on the island. Her whole face shone with happiness.

"You've got the job," Barbie told her.

Winnie's smile grew even brighter. "You don't know how wonderful it feels to move. I should have started swimming right away. I feel so free, so wonderful."

Barbie felt herself smiling, too. "Come on back to the island and rest until the show starts. Remember, thumbs down is the signal if you need help."

"Oh, I won't need any," Winnie assured her, just before diving back into the water.

When they got back to shore, Midge and Kira were standing in the surf waiting. "How did it go?" Kira asked as she and Midge helped Winnie into her wheelchair.

"She's great. She can do it," Barbie replied.

"All right!" Kira cheered. "Way to go, Winnie!"

"How's Jazzie?" Barbie asked.

"She feels pretty bad," said Midge, "but so far, I don't think we have to rush her to the hospital or anything like that."

They wheeled Winnie onto the beach. Teresa sponged the bright colors into the girl's hair. When they were all in their mermaid costumes with their hair done, Barbie handed them each a pink coral shell necklace. "I found these in town and thought they would be nice. They're for good luck," she told them.

"We have a special gift for you, too," said Midge. She reached into her canvas tote bag and pulled out a package wrapped in pink tissue paper. "Here," she said.

Barbie pulled apart the string. "Oh, wow!" she cried when it was open. "A pink mermaid tail!" She held the costume out in front of her. "Just like in my dream."

"I found the material the other day in a store," Midge explained.

"Thanks, you guys," said Barbie. At that moment, she saw the *Island Lady* coming into view. "All right, everyone get into the water. It's show time!"

9

Show Time!

Just as they had planned, Alex kept the customers busy by giving them a talk about the history of Mermaid Island. While he spoke, Barbie and her friends swam silently out to the boat and gathered at the front of it.

Just when Alex was about to open up the door revealing the glass bottom, Steve threw a string bag of conch meat into the water. That was the signal for the show to begin.

"Are you OK?" Barbie checked with Winnie as the string bag splashed into the water in front of her.

"Great," Winnie smiled. Yet Barbie worried that she looked tired. It had to be difficult swimming without the full use of her legs.

"Remember, thumbs down if you have trouble," Barbie reminded her.

Quickly, Barbie handed out the conch and then, all at the same time, the mermaids dove down under the boat. While they waited for the rays, the mermaids did their circle dance. Barbie kept a sharp eye on Winnie, looking for any sign of a problem. But the girl danced prettily, her dark eyes bright and her black hair floating around her like a true mermaid.

In minutes, the manta rays began to come forward for their feeding. When Barbie surfaced for air, she could hear the crowd on the boat murmuring with delight. She also heard the tape of their concert playing in the background.

Ken leaned over the side of the boat. "They love this show so much. Is the air pipe working?"

"It's great, but Kira was using it so I came up," Barbie explained. "Are the kids frightened of the rays?"

"In a fun way—the kind of scared you feel at a haunted house," Ken replied.

"How does Alex feel about Winnie swimming?" she asked.

"He hasn't seen her yet. He's been really busy with the customers and hasn't even looked at the show."

"I'd better get back down there," Barbie said, taking a big gulp of air.

She got down as the mermaids were just getting into a line. Barbie got to the head of the line. At her signal, all the mermaids flipped forward at once into a circle.

After several more moves, all of them came above the water. The customers on the boat rushed over to the side to see them. At that moment, Alan turned on the stereo. The tape that he played was a musical set Barbie and the gang had played at the concert. Now, the mermaids sang a song to the music. It was a song Barbie and Kira had written.

"Island breeze singing in the trees," they sang out as they waved to the customers. "Mermaids swim in the aqua seas. The joys of island life are these."

As Barbie continued singing, she looked up at Alex who had come out onto the front deck of the boat. At that moment, he looked down at the water and froze. Obviously, he had spotted Winnie. His face lit with happiness. Barbie wasn't sure, but she thought she saw tears of joy come to his eyes. She looked over at Winnie. Her face was radiant as she sang out in a lovely, crystal-clear voice.

"Island waves, island sun," the mermaids sang. "Days of laughter, days of fun. And the best days have just begun."

Slowly, the boat pulled away just as they had planned. The mermaids waved to the customers, who waved back at them. Barbie had never seen such happy smiles. She was thrilled that their show had given the customers so much joy.

Slowly, Barbie and her friends swam back to Mermaid Island. Jazzie was on the shore to greet them. "How do you feel?" Barbie asked.

"A lot better," Jazzie said.

Winnie sat in the shallow surf, looking out at the ocean. She had a faraway expression on her face. "What are you thinking?" Barbie asked her.

"That I wish I really was a mermaid," Winnie answered.

"It is a wonderful fantasy," Barbie agreed.

In a half-hour, Steve arrived in a motorboat to take them back to the main island. "You ladies had better rest," he told them. "Word has already spread that the mermaid show is the greatest thing ever. Alex wants to know if you're up to doing another performance."

Barbie looked at her friends questioningly. "I am," said Midge. The others agreed that they could perform again, too.

"Good!" cried Jazzie, "Now I'll get to perform, after all."

"How about you, Winnie?" Barbie asked.

"I feel fine, better than fine," she said. "I haven't had this much fun in months. But are there enough costumes?"

"Sure," Kira said. "Since we made the extra pink costume for Barbie there's one left over. Now it's yours."

"A six-mermaid show is even better than a five-mermaid show," said Christie.

"OK, you mermaids," Steve called to them. "Come on back for a little rest and relaxation because pretty soon it will once again be..."

"Show time!" the friends shouted happily together as they wiggled out of their costumes and climbed aboard the motorboat.

10

Saying Good-bye

"And it says on your application that you're a good swimmer," Barbie spoke to the young woman in front of her.

"I've been swimming since I was a girl."

"Great," said Barbie. "Go see Winnie and Kira over there on the dock. They'll tell you about the swimming try-out. You've passed this part of the interview."

The woman smiled. "Oh, thank you. This sounds like the job of my dreams."

"Thank you for coming down to see us," Barbie said.

As the woman went to see Kira and Winnie, Barbie adjusted her pink sun visor and looked at the line of other women who had come down to the marina to apply for jobs as *Island Lady* mermaids. Since Barbie and the gang would be leaving the next morning, she had to find new mermaids to take their place in the fantastically popular *Island Lady* Mermaid Show. Barbie had been interviewing and reading applications since the day before— as well as performing in two mermaid shows a day.

Alex came off his boat and walked up the dock toward her. "Good news," he said. "I've been going over my reservations and I'll need to add a third show to my schedule."

"Does that mean you'll want six more mermaids?" Barbie asked.

"Yes, I think so," Alex agreed. "I don't want any of my mermaids getting overtired. Not everyone can work as hard as you and your friends have worked this week. Thanks to you, I'll be finished paying for this boat much more quickly than I would have ever dreamed. I even have money left over to send Winnie to physical therapy three times a week."

"Seeing Winnie smile again has been one of the best parts of this whole thing," Barbie said fondly.

"The doctors can't believe the change in her," Alex said. "Swimming every day as a mermaid has done wonders for her leg muscles, and for her spirits."

"Since she's now in charge of the mermaid show, she'll be swimming more than ever," Barbie pointed out. "Now I think you'd better let me get back to these future mermaids. I don't want to leave them standing in the hot sun for too long."

Barbie spent the rest of the day interviewing new mermaids for the show. Then she helped out with the swimming audition which was held on the beach behind Alex's house. The sun was beginning to set over the water when Barbie announced the names of the eighteen mermaids and the six back-up mermaids she and the gang had picked. "Thank you all for coming. All mermaids meet Winnie on the dock tomorrow. She will teach you what to do."

"It's been a long day," said Christie. "But I think we got the best mermaids for the job."

At that moment, Alex came down to the beach dressed in white pants and a blue sports jacket. "All of you have exactly one half-hour to dress up in party clothes and be on the *Island Lady*," he announced.

"What's going on?" asked Teresa.

"You'll see," Alex replied mysteriously.

Barbie and the gang raced up to the house and quickly changed. Barbie wore a waisted pink dress with a glittery top and a billowy satin skirt. She braided her hair on one side and then finished the look with her glitter makeup. The rest of the gang looked great, too. Kira had on a great slim blue dress with a festive tie-dye skirt that flared at her knees. Teresa wore a flowered sundress.

Before long, they were on the *Island Lady* heading out to sea. "Isn't this the way to Angel's Food?" Barbie asked after a short while.

"It is, indeed," Alex replied. When they neared Angel's place the gang gasped all at once. The palm trees were strung with lanterns and a band played near the water. "I invited a few friends to a party in your honor," Alex told them as he anchored at Angel's dock.

Angel was there to greet them. "Welcome," she said. "Come, eat, dance, have a good time. You've earned it."

The gang did exactly that. "This has been some vacation," said Midge as the group stood together near the band. "I'll be sad to go. I'm not ready for the cold winter back home."

"Actually," Barbie said, "I love winter in the city. I won't mind sitting in front of the fireplace and reading a good book."

Kira laughed. "Barbie, you're amazing. You can even find the bright side of blizzard season."

Just then, Alex quieted the band. "I have an announcement," he said. "I have just asked Angel to marry me and she has said yes!"

Everyone at the party cheered, especially Barbie and her friends. "And now I have an announcement," said Winnie, coming up beside her father. "I want everyone to raise their cups high to toast Barbie."

Barbie smiled as everyone at the party raised their cups. But she felt happier still when she saw Winnie take her father's arm and get to her feet. Wobbling a little, Winnie took a shaky step forward and raised her cup. "To Barbie," she said, "who really knows how to make dreams come true!"

Barbie put her arm around Winnie and hugged her as the crowd toasted: "To Barbie! Hurray!"